More Munsch to Enjoy!

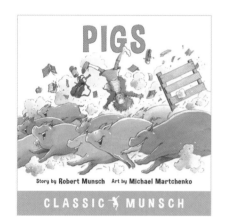

PIGS

Story by **Robert Munsch** Art by **Michael Martchenko**

CLASSIC MUNSCH

PURPLE, GREEN AND YELLOW

Story by **Robert Munsch** Art by **Hélène Desputeaux**

CLASSIC MUNSCH

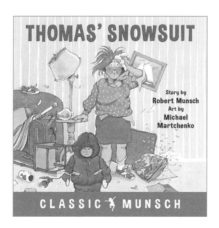

THOMAS' SNOWSUIT

Story by **Robert Munsch** Art by **Michael Martchenko**

CLASSIC MUNSCH

STEPHANIE'S PONYTAIL

Story by **Robert Munsch** Art by **Michael Martchenko**

CLASSIC MUNSCH

The
Paper Bag Princess

The Paper Bag Princess

STORY by
ROBERT MUNSCH

ART by
MICHAEL MARTCHENKO

annick press
toronto • berkeley

We acknowledge the support of the Canada Council for the Arts and the Ontario Arts Council, and the participation of the Government of Canada/la participation du gouvernement du Canada for our publishing activities.

Library and Archives Canada Cataloguing in Publication

Munsch, Robert N., 1945-, author
    The paper bag princess / Robert Munsch ; illustrated by Michael
Martchenko. -- Classic Munsch edition.

Originally published in 1980.
ISBN 978-1-77321-030-8 (hardcover).--ISBN 978-1-77321-029-2 (softcover)

    I. Martchenko, Michael, illustrator II. Title.

PS8576.U575P36 2018   jC813'.54   C2017-905736-7

Published in the U.S.A. by Annick Press (U.S.) Ltd.
Distributed in Canada by University of Toronto Press.
Distributed in the U.S.A. by Publishers Group West.

Printed in China

www.annickpress.com
www.robertmunsch.com

Also available in e-book format.
Please visit www.annickpress.com/ebooks.html for more details.

To Elizabeth

Elizabeth was a beautiful princess.
She lived in a castle and had expensive
princess clothes. She was going to marry
a prince named Ronald.

Unfortunately, a dragon smashed her castle,
burned all her clothes with his fiery breath,
and carried off Prince Ronald.

Elizabeth decided to chase the dragon and get Ronald back.

She looked everywhere for something to wear, but the only thing she could find that was not burnt was a paper bag. So she put on the paper bag and followed the dragon.

He was easy to follow, because he left a trail of burnt forests and horses' bones.

Finally, Elizabeth came to a cave with a large door that had a huge knocker on it. She took hold of the knocker and banged on the door.

The dragon stuck his nose out of the door and said, "Well, a princess! I love to eat princesses, but I have already eaten a whole castle today. I am a very busy dragon. Come back tomorrow."

He slammed the door so fast that Elizabeth almost got her nose caught.

Elizabeth grabbed the knocker and banged on the door again.

The dragon stuck his nose out of the door and said, "Go away. I love to eat princesses, but I have already eaten a whole castle today. I am a very busy dragon. Come back tomorrow."

"Wait," shouted Elizabeth. "Is it true that you are the smartest and fiercest dragon in the whole world?"

"Yes," said the dragon.

"Is it true," said Elizabeth, "that you can burn up ten forests with your fiery breath?"

"Oh, yes," said the dragon, and he took a huge, deep breath and breathed out so much fire that he burnt up fifty forests.

"Fantastic," said Elizabeth, and the dragon took another huge breath and breathed out so much fire that he burnt up one hundred forests.

"Magnificent," said Elizabeth, and the dragon took another huge breath, but this time nothing came out. The dragon didn't even have enough fire left to cook a meatball.

Elizabeth said, "Dragon, is it true that you can fly around the world in just ten seconds?"

"Why, yes," said the dragon, and jumped up and flew all the way around the world in just ten seconds.

He was very tired when he got back, but Elizabeth shouted, "Fantastic, do it again!"

So the dragon jumped up and flew around the whole world in just twenty seconds.

When he got back he was too tired to talk, and he lay down and went straight to sleep.

Elizabeth whispered, very softly, "Hey, dragon." The dragon didn't move at all.

She lifted up the dragon's ear and put her head right inside. She shouted as loud as she could, "Hey, dragon!"

The dragon was so tired he didn't even move.

Elizabeth walked right over the dragon and opened the door to the cave.

There was Prince Ronald. He looked at her and said, "Elizabeth, you are a mess! You smell like ashes, your hair is all tangled, and you are wearing a dirty old paper bag. Come back when you are dressed like a real princess."

"Ronald," said Elizabeth, "your clothes are really pretty and your hair is very neat. You look like a real prince, but you are a bum."

They didn't get married after all.

Even More Classic Munsch:

The Dark
Mud Puddle
The Boy in the Drawer
Jonathan Cleaned Up, Then He Heard a Sound
Millicent and the Wind
Mortimer
The Fire Station
Angela's Airplane
David's Father
Thomas' Snowsuit
50 Below Zero
I Have to Go!
Moira's Birthday
A Promise is a Promise
Pigs
Something Good
Show and Tell
Purple, Green and Yellow
Wait and See
Where is Gah-Ning?
From Far Away
Stephanie's Ponytail
Munschworks: The First Munsch Collection
Munschworks 2: The Second Munsch Treasury
Munschworks 3: The Third Munsch Treasury
Munschworks 4: The Fourth Munsch Treasury
The Munschworks Grand Treasury
Munsch Mini-Treasury One
Munsch Mini-Treasury Two
Munsch Mini-Treasury Three

For information on these titles please visit www.annickpress.com
Many Munsch titles are available in French and/or Spanish, as well as in
board book and e-book editions. Please contact your favorite supplier.

More Munsch to Enjoy!

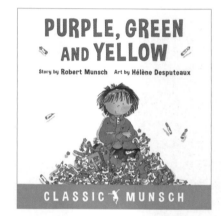

PURPLE, GREEN AND YELLOW

Story by Robert Munsch   Art by Hélène Desputeaux

CLASSIC ✦ MUNSCH

PIGS

Story by Robert Munsch   Art by Michael Martchenko

CLASSIC ✦ MUNSCH

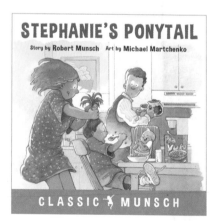

STEPHANIE'S PONYTAIL

Story by Robert Munsch   Art by Michael Martchenko

CLASSIC ✦ MUNSCH

THOMAS' SNOWSUIT

Story by Robert Munsch
Art by Michael Martchenko

CLASSIC ✦ MUNSCH